D0291585

THE OPTION

THE OPTION

HERMAN BROWN

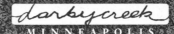

MINNEAPOLIS

Darby Creek
A division of Lerner Publishing Group, Inc.
241 First Avenue North
Minneapolis, MN 55401 USA

For reading levels and more information, look up this title
at www.lernerbooks.com.

Main body text set in Janson Text LT Std 12/17.
Typeface provided by Linotype AG.

Front cover: © Mike Powell/CORBIS. Backgrounds: © iStockphoto.com/
mack2happy, (grass).

Library of Congress Cataloging-in-Publication Data

Brown, Herman 1971–
        The option / by Herman Brown.
            pages   cm. — (The red zone ; #3)
        Summary: The Central High Trojan's star quarterback, Shane, was
    arrested for drunk driving and Coach Z may have covered up, so when
    Shane gets in trouble again, back-up quarterback Gary must decide whether
    to expose them both.
        ISBN 978–1–4677–2128–8 (lib. bdg. : alk. paper)
        ISBN 978–1–4677–4651–9 (eBook)
        [1. Football—Fiction. 2. High schools—Fiction. 3. Schools—Fiction.
    4. Drunk driving—Fiction. 5. Conduct of life—Fiction.] I. Title.
    PZ7.B737757Opt 2014
    [Fic]—dc23   2013046619

Manufactured in the United States of America
1 – SB – 7/15/14

1/FRIDAY, SEPTEMBER 20—
PARTY AT DEVON'S HOUSE

I got it. I paid for it with a dislocated jaw and a severely damaged ego, but I got it. I got the video.

The proof.

Coach Zachary would have to listen to me now. And he'd have to do the right thing. Or else.

"Dude," Orlando said, smiling. "You got your butt *kicked*." Orlando Green, Troy Central

High's star wide receiver, had big talent, a bigger ego, and an even bigger mouth.

"Chut uck," I said. My dangling jaw made it hard to say shut up. I held the jaw with one hand while clutching my smartphone in the other. That phone had the precious footage on it.

"You gotta get to the ER," Ernie Erickson said. He was a varsity tight end, but he wasn't a big shot like Orlando and a lot of the other guys. He didn't get all caught up in the mythology around Troy football. He believed in the game, but he knew it was only one part of life—not *life*.

The crowd that had gathered in the yard to watch the fight was drifting away. Onlookers headed back inside the house to the party. Someone changed the music and cranked it up—some kind of metal. A few blocks away, tires squealed and horns honked. That would be Shane Hunter, the starting QB and the star of my video, swerving through the streets of Troy.

I realized my head was pounding.

"Yeah," I said to Ernie. "I khink you wight."

"What you gotta do," said Orlando, "is erase that video. Now." He reached for the phone in my hand, but Ernie grabbed his wrist.

"Step off, O."

Orlando got up in his face. "Who you think you talking to?"

Ernie gave him his meanest game face and puffed up his big chest. He was an imposing guy. Orlando was tough, but even with his ego, he knew he didn't stand a chance in a fight with Ernie. Nobody did.

"You better go inside," Ernie said in a voice like Clint Eastwood. "Or else we'll have to find out just how tough you are." Just to make sure Orlando got his point, he added, "I will turn you into a stain on this driveway."

I was glad Ernie was on *my* side.

Orlando stared Ernie down for a few seconds, enough to convince himself he didn't look like a total wimp. But then he went inside as he was told. Ernie and I climbed into his dad's pickup and took off for the hospital.

"Chanks," I said, still holding up my jaw. I wanted to puke, it hurt so bad. But puking would hurt even worse.

"Don't worry about it," he said. He glanced over at me. "I just hope it was worth it."

At that point, I wasn't sure it was. I pulled up the video on my phone. Shane stood swaying on the screen, a plastic tumbler of OJ and vodka in his hand, just after hitting me in the face so hard that I saw stars. I was surprised you couldn't see them circling my head on screen, like in cartoons.

In my defense, Shane didn't look so hot either. Bloody nose, black eye. I think he spilled some of his drink, too, which probably hurt him more than anything else.

"You got nothing, *backup*!" he yelled. "Nothing! You can practice twenty-four hours a day for the rest of your life, and you'll always be my backup. You'll be backing me up on the nursing home team."

He wiped his mouth with the back of his hand and laughed at the blood that came off on his wrist. His eyes dared me to say something else. But his gaze was loose and unfocused. "Always gonna be second best, Gary."

He turned and stumbled off the curb before getting into his Chevy. The tires squealed, and he took off.

Everything was as clear as can be. Shane had been drinking, which he'd promised Coach he wouldn't do. And then he'd been driving—which he'd already been busted for once. That was a district violation and, more important, a team violation. Once Coach Z saw this, Shane would be benched, maybe even suspended.

And I'd be the starter.

"Yeah," I said to Ernie. "It yuzh earch it."

2/MONDAY, AUGUST 19—
TROJANS FOOTBALL PRACTICE

I've always been Shane's backup. Even in Troy's Half Backs kids' football camp. We were good buddies back then, and it never bothered me that Shane was the best and I was second best. Football was just a game. It was something us kids did together for fun, just like baseball and soccer. Just like Legos and video games and climbing trees. Just like damming up the creek one rainy day so that our army man war zone got flooded and we played out a muddy battle. That battle was awesome. We pushed our plastic tanks through the muck. We set up ambushes along the river, with army men hiding in the branches attacking enemy army men that rafted down the stream. I still consider that day one of the most fun of my life.

But even then, we sensed that football was something more for everyone else in town. Especially those adults who'd grown up here. Trojan football wasn't a game for them.

By the time we reached middle school, people started paying a lot more attention to Shane. They knew he had the talent to be a star. In eighth grade, I heard people saying he could get a full ride to Ohio State—or anywhere. Seriously.

The legend began to grow. Shane could throw a football that hit a jackrabbit at full sprint eighty yards away. Shane could outrun a cougar. Shane could bench press a grizzly bear.

No wonder his head got so pumped up with pride. No wonder he couldn't see the fun in this kid's game anymore.

And just to be clear: I was good. Dad said I'd be starting on any other team in the division, and he was right. I'd seen lots of other QBs come through town over the years, and I knew I could have beaten them out. When Shane was starter on the varsity team as a freshman, I ran JV. We went undefeated while Shane and the rest of varsity were taking their lumps.

Now that we were seniors, everyone said we had a shot at the state title. Even Coach Z thought so, though he wouldn't admit it. You start looking more than one game ahead, you lose focus. That's what he's always said. And I believed him.

Anyway, here I was backing up Shane again, just like when we were little kids in Half Backs. But unlike our Half Backs days, he rode me all practice. "Yo, backup, watch how it's done!" he'd say. "Hey backup, get me a water."

With the attitude came the drinking, and

you could tell Shane wasn't having fun playing. All he cared about was winning, partying, and Ohio State.

Any trace of the kid he used to be was long gone.

Last summer, something changed. Shane showed up to practice so hungover he couldn't get through the reps. Then he did it again a week later. That was cool, because I got his reps. I don't mind saying it: I looked good. I even thought I could beat him out.

Yeah, I was fooling myself. I couldn't beat him out, even on my best day. But I started getting the itch.

Then, just a few days before the first game, he missed practice. First time ever. Well, all right, I thought. That was the kind of crap that Coach Z would not put up with. I was going to get my shot.

Next day, Shane shows up like nothing happened. But here's what's even weirder:

Coach also acted like nothing happened. Shane played with the first team, and I was second string. Same as ever.

But even if Coach wasn't talking about what happened, the team was. Shane had been busted for driving under the influence. He hadn't been at practice because he had been in jail.

After practice, I came up to Coach while the rest of the guys headed for the locker room.

"What's up, Jayo?"

I was supposed to feel good because he called me by my last name. Most second stringers? Coach Z just referred to them by number. *Hey, 54! You gotta make that tackle!* Stuff like that. But he respected me. He knew I could go live with my mom in Harvest Valley and start for them. But Dad needed me here. That's why I stayed.

"Coach, I was wondering, you know, since Shane missed practice yesterday, I know that's one of your Golden Commandments. Probably the biggest one. So, anyway, I was wondering if since he missed, you know, I would be starting

Friday." God, Coach Z made me nervous. I hated the way I sounded when talking to him. Like a nervous little boy.

Coach cocked his head at me and spat on the grass. I squinted into the sun and the blazing fire of his authority.

"You let me be the coach, all right, Jayo?"

"Well, yeah, but, I mean, of course. But, you know, it's one of the Golden Commandments. I thought that was unbreakable." I was sweating more now than I had during practice.

"I'm gonna tell you this one more time," he said, "I'm the coach of this team, and I will make the decisions about who plays. You got a problem with that?"

"No," I said softly. "No problem, sir. Sorry."

"All right then."

Coach started to walk toward the locker room. I just stood there. It started to burn me up. All that garbage about how there's no *I* in team, how you have to respect the game, how if you break one of Coach's Golden Commandments, you sit—all that was just BS. At least it was if you were Shane Hunter.

I ran to catch up with him.

"Coach!"

He stopped, but he didn't turn around.

"Coach," I said. "I know why Shane missed. I think you know too."

He turned to me. I waited for him to say something, but he just stared me down. We stood like that for a few seconds. My knees started to shake, but I didn't back down.

Finally he said, "I don't know what rumors are flying around, son, but I guarantee you don't know the whole story. Remember this: everybody deserves a second chance."

Really? That wasn't the message he usually sent. Usually it was "My way or the highway."

"We through here?" he asked.

"Yes, sir."

And he went inside.

3/MONDAY, SEPTEMBER 16—
BEFORE SCHOOL

One Monday a few weeks later, after we'd won our third game to get to a two–one record, I woke up to the sound of my dad throwing up in the bathroom again. He didn't just make some normal puke sound. When Dad had one of these days, you could hear him all the way down the block. His body would twist itself into a knot trying to get every last bit of his insides out.

I had to pee pretty badly, but I knew he could be a while, so I went in the backyard. I'm not proud of it, but I'd done it before. When your dad is on the kind of meds that scrape the core out of your body, certain life changes come your way. Peeing in the grass is a small one.

I went back inside and measured out some oatmeal and water into a bowl and stuck it in the microwave. Dad would be hungry when he was done, and oatmeal was about the only thing he could hold down. I'd become a decent cook since Mom left, but sometimes, the simple things were all the situation called for.

The microwave beeped. I pulled out the bowl and stirred in some brown sugar and cream, just like Dad liked it. A few minutes later, he came into the kitchen and inhaled deeply, like he was smelling something special instead of the same old thing.

"Ah," he said in a big fake Italian accent, "oatmeal à la Gary especialamento!"

Dad was always trying to be funny and complimentary and everything. He hoped that through all this goofing around and buddy-buddy stuff we did, like going to the clinic together, I would stop being mad at him for cheating on Mom. For getting HIV from that woman in Columbus and breaking up our family.

But it wasn't his true self. All his acting did was remind me—as if I needed a reminder—how important it is to do the right thing in life. Be true to yourself, do what you say you'll do. And then you don't have to act like a doofus to try to win your son's love.

Besides, I was already here. I'd chosen him. What more did he want?

"Sounded like a rough one this morning, Dad."

"It wasn't a pleasure cruise, that's for sure. You working tonight?"

"Swing shift," I said.

I started bussing tables at Café Helen last year after Mom left to live in Harvest Valley with her sister. Money became really tight really fast, especially with Dad missing out on work. He was usually too sick to plow snow or cut lawns. Not to mention all his meds added a strain to the budget.

I made decent tips down at the café. But it wasn't always easy to balance a job, school, homework, and football. Now that I was a senior and still not starting, I sometimes felt like sports weren't worth it. Sometimes I wondered why I stayed on the team.

"Well, don't miss practice, son."

Oh, yeah. That was why: Dad. He'd be heartbroken if I gave up the game. He'd played when he went to Troy High, and he expected me to play, too. He was one of those people who believed the mythology of Trojan football. It was *life*.

Even though I was mad at him, and even though I did *not* think Trojan football was *life*, I couldn't let him down. He was such a mess without Mom. He needed something to believe in. One thing he believed—foolishly—was that

I could beat out Shane and start for the Trojans. He felt that favoritism had allowed Shane to start over me.

"Don't worry, Dad," I said, grabbing my gear on my way to the door. "I won't miss."

"Hold on," he said, stirring his oatmeal. "I'm trying to tell you something. I got a feeling they're going to need you on the field this week."

"What do you mean?"

"Just something I heard yesterday cutting the graveyard. From Bailey."

Alfred Bailey was his boss on the yard crew. He was on the Friends of Troy Football boosters too, and he had a way of nosing into everything. Always plugged into the gossip.

"What?" I asked.

"You remember a few weeks ago when Shane got arrested?"

"How could I forget?"

"Well, the word is that Principal Donahue found out that Coach Z was covering up for him. Could be some trouble coming downstream—and some opportunities."

I was stunned. Coach Z was an Important Man, capital *I*, capital *M*. He'd played on the only undefeated Trojans team in school history, and now he was leading us to a state championship—so he believed. And so everyone else believed. It was hard to imagine trouble coming downstream for him. Not now. Not ever.

"Wow," I said.

"Yeah," he said. "Wow. Now knock 'em dead today."

4/MONDAY, SEPTEMBER 16—
TROY CENTRAL HIGH

Pulling into the school parking lot in Dad's Honda, I saw Shane and Orlando near the back of the lot. I parked next to them and rapped on the window of Shane's Chevy. Shane rolled it down.

"What up, Two?" He meant QB2. As in, backup.

"Have you heard anything about Coach?" I asked.

"Heard what? What're you talking about?" Orlando handed him a plastic water bottle full of orange juice. And vodka, I assumed. Shane took a swig. Even his hands had bulging muscles.

"Uh, nothing," I said. "Just, you know, just wondering if you heard anything."

"I don't know what you're talking about, but I ain't heard a thing."

"OK, cool. Talk to you later."

"Hold up, Two," Shane said. "You want a drink?" He handed me the jug.

"No, I'm good."

Orlando leaned in front of Shane. "Yeah, you are good, aren't you? Such a good boy. Such a mama's boy. Whoops, I guess not, since you got no mama around, huh?"

He and Shane laughed pretty hard at that. Then Shane hit a button on his stereo and Eminem came cranking out. I never understood how he had his own ride and an awesome stereo while his family was dirt poor. No money, lousy grades, no anything—except football.

Actually, I had an idea. Illegal gifts from college recruiters.

"Classy," I said over the music and started to walk away. Then Shane turned it down again.

"Hey," he said, "why didn't you come to the party Friday? It was a rager."

"I don't know," I said.

"Everyone was asking about you."

"Really?"

"No," he said and took a drink. "They weren't."

I left them laughing there and went into the school.

5/MONDAY, SEPTEMBER 16— PRACTICE AND SWING SHIFT AT CAFÉ HELEN

That afternoon, Coach was pretty grumpy and made us run double laps to open practice. Other than that, nothing was different. He had Shane run the first-team offense, and I got the scraps.

I appealed to Coach Whitson, the offensive coach. "Don't I need some more reps? What if Shane can't start Friday?"

Whitson, who always looked confused, gave me a more dumbfounded look than usual. "Why wouldn't Shane start Friday?"

"Well . . ."

But he didn't have the slightest idea what I was talking about. That was clear. So I dropped it. And I had to hand it to Shane, he was throwing lasers, hitting every target. How did he do it when he had been drinking at eight in the morning?

When I got in, I was throwing pretty well too. I hit Orlando in stride on a long post, but he dropped it.

"Gotta hold tight to those!" Coach Whitson yelled.

"Bit more wobble on it than I'm used to," Orlando said, winking at me.

"Let's try it again," Whitson said. "Jayo, lay it in there this time."

Was he serious?

Meanwhile, Shane and Coach Z were reviewing something on a clipboard. My next pass was short and got picked off.

"Come on, Two!" Shane yelled.

God, I hated him.

Coach Z came to Café Helen that night and sat at the counter. I was surprised, but not because he showed up. It was the only decent restaurant in town, and he had been there before. I was surprised because usually when I saw him out he was with his wife. He was alone this time. He ordered French onion soup and a tall beer. When I came to take away his dirty bowl, he grabbed my arm.

"I hear you've been making noises about Shane not being able to start. Again."

"I was just asking, Coach. I want to play, you know that."

"You need to get comfortable with your role on this team," Coach Z said. "You're not helping us win games if you're stirring up trouble."

"I don't mean to stir up trouble, Coach." I lowered my voice to a whisper. "I'm the one who's stayed *out* of trouble!"

He thought about that for a second. "Look," he said. "I know you and Shane have a history. I know you want to play. I appreciate that. But if I hear about you shooting off your mouth again about this stuff, you *will* regret it. I'll see to that."

He took out his wallet and dropped a twenty on the counter. Then he scooted off his stool and left.

"It's impressive," Dad said that night. We sat on the couch watching TV. He was streaming some documentary about freshwater sharks, and I had told him how the trouble Alfred Bailey predicted never made it downstream. Coach Z had no intention of benching Shane, and there was no sign that Principal Donahue or anyone else was going to do anything about it.

"Impressive?" I said. "That's not the word that came to my mind. More like infuriating.

More like—this is stupid."

"That's three words."

"Well, it's not impressive."

"Zachary is even more protected than I thought," Dad said. "I mean, I knew this town loves him. I knew he was safe. But this—this is impressive."

"And from now on, he can be impressive without me on the team," I said. "I'm done with this."

We watched the TV for a few minutes more, but I could tell Dad was thinking. He wasn't going to let a statement like that linger for very long. On screen, a guy held a shark about two feet long in his hands. "I need to hold on tight here," the guy said. "He'll take a big ol' bite out of me if he has half a chance."

"Maybe," Dad said, "it's time to go on the attack."

6/FRIDAY, SEPTEMBER 20—
AWAY GAME VS. THE TIGERS

"Yo, Ernie!" Shane said, walking toward us in the hall after school. "You best pack a lunch tonight, bro. Don't let me down."

Our opponent the next night was the West High Tigers, a team known to be very physical—and dirty. They'd poke at your eyes, chop block, you name it. And they had a couple very big, very fast defensive ends, which meant

Shane would be facing more pressure than he'd faced...maybe ever. It also meant Ernie would get a lot more snaps, because Coach Z wanted the tight end to help block on every down.

Instead of getting conservative, like most teams that played the Tigers, we planned an air raid: lots of passes. That put a lot of pressure on Ernie and the rest of the line to keep Shane upright.

Shane was as excited as I'd ever seen him. He rubbed his big hands together like a B-movie villain. "All of Ohio will be watching us after tonight, boys," he said. "It's gonna be a wake-up call."

"Don't worry about me," Ernie said. "I'm up for this."

Shane turned to me. "What up, Two? You ready to learn something?"

"Whatever, man," I said.

"No, seriously. I'll be putting on a clinic."

"Yeah?" I said. "I think you're putting on a clinic in how to, like, not have rules apply to you!"

"That's the stupidest thing I've ever heard, Two."

"Well, too bad."

"'Too bad?' Are you serious right now? You sound like a preschooler."

Which was true. I said stupid stuff sometimes when I got nervous or angry.

Shane shook his head. "Hey, maybe if you were more of a man, your dad wouldn't have turned to an 'alternative lifestyle.' Maybe he wouldn't have AIDS."

"He has HIV," I said. "Not AIDS."

Shane just laughed. I wanted to punch him—knock the pride out of his voice. But I didn't have the courage. I never got in fights, and I knew I'd get my butt kicked. As Shane walked away, fist-bumping other guys on the team, Ernie said, "Wow, what a creep."

Then I had an idea.

"Ernie," I said. "Want to do me a favor?"

Near the end of the first half of the Tigers game, Coach Z's plan was working pretty well. Shane was already thirteen for sixteen, with two TD passes and a couple big scrambles. Ernie and the guys were doing a great job of keeping him clean, and Coach Z was calling screens, slants, outs—even a couple bombs. The Tigers D-line was getting frustrated— they weren't used to being manhandled like that. You could hear them bicker with each other between plays.

We were in the Tigers' house, and we were in their heads too. Everything was clicking for us.

With only a few ticks left on the clock before the half, Coach Z called for a draw. We had a good lead, and he was playing it safe with time running down. Plus, maybe we could spring Devon, the running back. The Tigers hadn't seen much of him all game.

But Shane got greedy. He called an audible at the line, Orlando ran a post, and Shane launched it his way—into a swarm. A defensive end got a fingernail on Shane's elbow as he threw, the ball came out a tiny bit wrong, and it got picked off. The safety ran it all the way back as time expired, and we went into the locker room up only seventeen–seven instead of seventeen–zero.

"What were you thinking, Hunter?" Coach said. "There were three DBs back there! You think you're invincible? You don't throw into triple coverage!"

"Sorry, Coach, I thought I had him. Orlando and me had something good going all night. I thought I had him."

"Listen," Coach said, "when we have four seconds before the half and a seventeen-point lead, you need to run the play I call. Got that?"

"Got it, Coach."

Coach had good things to say to everyone else—especially Ernie.

"Erickson, your guy hasn't even sniffed the backfield all night. I think he's gonna have a seizure out there if you keep shutting him down like that. I'd like to see that, actually. Keep it up."

Ernie nodded, and Coach continued.

"Gentlemen, listen. We're up by ten. This

is a Tigers team that thinks it has a shot at winning the division. They don't understand that it's *our* division. They're over there feeling pretty good—after that pick-six, they're in this thing. They're gonna come out hungry. Let's not let them get any momentum back, boys. Let's go out there and show them whose division it is!"

The Tigers had possession at the start of the second half. They ran a long, methodical drive that took up half the quarter: a halfback run off-tackle for six yards. A weak-side sweep for eight. QB keeper for six. After they got the TD, it was a three-point game.

"Let's get it back, boys!" Shane yelled after we took the kickoff out to the twenty-eight yard line.

Ernie gave me a slight nod as the offense took the field. Coach called a pitch to Devon that got us six yards, then a quick slant that got six more, and the Tiger defense got no pressure at all on Shane.

On first and ten, Coach called for a longer

pass. Shane went into a seven-step drop and looked downfield—until one of the big Tigers defensive ends flattened him.

Shane hit the ground with a thud, somehow holding onto the ball. The crowd exploded in cheers. The defensive end got up, howling and pumping his fist. Shane stayed down. Ernie stood with his hands on his hips, looking at the ground.

While Coach ran out to check on Shane, I grabbed a ball and started warming up with Brian Norwood, a linebacker. The Tigers defense was all high fives and laughter.

After a few seconds, Shane got up and started walking. The crowd applauded politely—they were impressed he was still breathing after that hit. Coach called me over and told me the play. A simple handoff to Devon, off-tackle.

I huddled the guys together, told them the play, and lined up under center. It felt good. The West High crowd was on its feet. They smelled blood. So did the Tigers defense, snarling and drooling like animals.

I took the snap and handed the ball to Devon, who ran into a brick wall. After losing eight yards on the sack, we lost two more on the botched run. All of a sudden, we were third and twenty on our own eighteen. It felt like the Tigers had all the momentum.

Coach called timeout, and we came off the field. Shane was playing catch with Brian. He looked fine.

"Shane's back in," Coach said, patting me on the head. He started telling the guys what play they'd run: a screen to Ernie. "We'll get a chunk of yards back and punt. The defense has to hold."

I was barely listening, though. My night was done.

As the team ran back onto the field and lined up, the West High crowd turned up the volume. Shane screamed out the snap count over the noise. I could see the steam of his angry breath all the way from the sideline.

As Shane dropped back, Ernie held his

block for a second and then released him. He stepped into the flat like he was supposed to, and it worked perfectly. He was wide open. But Shane didn't throw it. Instead, he ran directly toward the defensive end who Ernie had released, the same dude who had pounded him two plays earlier. He dodged to his right and threw a stiff-arm at the guy that left him grasping at air.

Once Shane burst around the line, Ernie picked up a block on the cornerback, and he kept on going. A safety hit him square in the hips, but Shane shook it off and picked up another six yards before another safety knocked him out of bounds. It was a twenty-six-yard gain: first down.

Shane smiled at the Tigers sideline as he trotted back to the huddle.

The next play, Shane changed Coach's call again and ran a QB draw right up the middle— into the teeth of the Tiger defense—and picked up nine yards. On second and one, Shane threw that post again, the one that got picked off at the end of the first half. Only this time, he dropped it into Orlando's arms. Orlando held the football like a baby as he ran all the way into the end zone.

The crowd was stunned. The Tigers were stunned. Coach was stunned.

Shane pointed to the defensive end who'd hit him earlier—a hit that seemed like it had happened hours ago—and winked. It was like he was saying, Nothing you do can stop me.

Nothing.

7/FRIDAY, SEPTEMBER 20—
PARTY AT DEVON'S HOUSE

Ernie and I went to the party that night at Devon's house. I was feeling pretty sorry for myself, even though we'd won thirty-four–ten. And I could tell that Ernie was ashamed at giving up that sack, which made me feel even worse. I'd asked him to do it. We decided we'd just show our faces for a few minutes and leave.

But right away, Shane started riding me.

"I hope you took notes, Two! I believe the scout from Ohio State took a few."

"Yeah, good game," I said. I was hoping to avoid a scene because Shane was a born scene-stealer. I knew I'd end up looking like a fool.

This girl Shawna was hanging all over Shane—like literally hanging onto his arm as if she was afraid he'd scramble away.

Shawna was not his girlfriend, by the way. Shane's girlfriend was Jenny. Shawna might have been the only girl in school who was hotter than her. Jenny and I were friends because we'd been on the video yearbook staff for three years. I happened to know that she was visiting her grandmother in Minnesota for the weekend.

Ernie and I started talking to some girls in the kitchen, but I couldn't concentrate. I kept thinking about Shane in the other room with Shawna. I kept thinking about all the crap he'd been shoveling at me for the past four years. And then I started thinking about that day we dammed up the creek for our army men, and I started getting kind of upset.

"What's the matter with you?"

This girl—her name was Becca—was glaring at me.

"Nothing," I said. "Sorry. Uh, why?"

"Because I asked you a question—like three times!"

"Sorry," I said. "The answer is yes."

Ernie and the girls laughed.

"Good," Ernie said. "You want to know the question?"

You could hear Orlando and Shane in the other room yelling some rah-rah stuff at each other. Stuff about how we're going to State this year, how unbeatable we are. Then Shane changed the music. I knew it was Shane because he put on Eminem. It was what he always played.

"The question was," Becca said, smiling now, "do you guys want to get out of here? I have some blankets in the car. Let's go to the lake."

"That sounds really good," I said. "I would *love* to get out of here."

I'd never spoken truer words. I couldn't wait to leave. And Becca was really sweet. We'd started flirting a couple weeks ago, but we hadn't gone out or anything—at least not yet.

But part of me was also making a plan. I was thinking, I wish I could show Jenny what Shane got up to while she was away. She should know how he was making a fool of her.

I wish I could say I was thinking only about Jenny's feelings, protecting her dignity. But the truth is I was mostly thinking of myself. I just wanted to get back at Shane.

The four of us left the kitchen and walked through the living room toward the front door. On our way through, I had my phone out—filming Shane and Shawna on the couch. Just as we were hitting the door, though, Shane saw me.

"What're you doing?"

He stood up. Shawna, whose legs were draped across his, fell onto the floor and dropped her bottle of beer.

I shoved the phone in my pocket as we

walked out the door. Shane caught up and grabbed my shoulder. "What was that all about?" He still had his drink with him. The ice clattered in the plastic tumbler.

"Nothing, QB1. Nothing at all."

"Give me your phone," Shane said.

"Nope."

"Give it to me now."

Becca took my hand. "Let's go," she said softly.

Instead, I punched Shane in the nose.

I don't know what came over me. All the weeks of frustration—all the *years* of frustration—bubbled over all at once.

Shane stumbled back. Anger coursed through me—it was like I wasn't in control of my body. I'd never felt that way before.

Shane set his drink down on a step. I came after him. As he looked up at me, I socked him in the eye. Becca and her friend screamed, and people poured out of the house to watch. I lunged at Shane again, but he was ready this time. He threw a fist into my gut that doubled me over.

I couldn't breathe. That was when Shane reached back and delivered a monster haymaker into my jaw that made me see stars.

Boom.

I crumpled onto the ground. Not only was Shane a better quarterback than me, he was a better fighter too. Which I should have predicted, since I'd never been in a fight. I knew he'd been in a lot of them over the years.

When I opened my eyes, he was standing over me. I thought he was going to kick me, but Ernie stepped in front of him.

Shane lost it. "You're just my backup!" he screamed. "You got nothing on me!"

It was like he couldn't believe somebody had dared to challenge him. By hitting him, I'd broken some kind of social agreement: Nobody was supposed to mess with him. Ever.

He was hysterical.

And, in all his anger, he seemed to have forgotten about the recording of him and Shawna. He kept screaming at me. Ernie kept on guard in case he attacked again. But it didn't seem like

Shane wanted to fight anymore. He was too far gone into his angry fit.

When Shane turned to pick up his drink, I pulled out my phone and started recording again. At that point, I didn't care if he beat me up. I didn't care if he stole the phone. I was all in. I was going to put an end to his crap.

He was going down.

8/SATURDAY, SEPTEMBER 21—
MORNING PAIN

The next morning, I felt terrible, but it wasn't only my dislocated jaw. Something else was eating at my insides.

Dad was throwing up in the bathroom again, which made me feel even worse. He'd had to come to the hospital and get me last night, when he should have been resting. I was so messed up I didn't even get up to make his oatmeal.

He came into my room later on. "I guess you'll miss practice, huh?"

I nodded. I wanted to say, "Who cares about practice?" but I had bandages wrapped around my head to keep the jaw from moving. The ER doctor had stuck her thumbs inside my mouth and popped the jaw back in place, which had hurt like crazy in spite of the painkillers.

Dad put a hand on my forehead, the sliver of it that showed through the bandages, and gave me a look. Was he sad that I was hurt? Was he disappointed I'd acted so immaturely last night? Did he feel bad about my childhood friendship dissolving into nothing? Or was it just that I was missing practice?

He made me a smoothie and stuck it in the refrigerator before he left for work. He had a big corporate campus to take care of that day. I was glad he felt up for it because I didn't want to sit around all day with him: two sick, messed-up, pitiful guys streaming nature shows on TV. It was too depressing to think about.

Surprisingly, the smoothie boosted my spirits quite a lot. I decided to go over and help Devon clean up his parents' house. After that party, he'd need the help. And maybe doing something positive would help me feel better about myself.

"Yo," Devon said when I came in. "Here he is: UFC champion Gary Jayo!"

"Very funny," I tried to say, but it came out *ggh-ghee huggee.*

"Take it easy, Jayo. I'll do the talking, OK?"

We grabbed black lawn bags from the garage and started filling them with cans, bottles, boxes, chip bags, fast food wrappers, and whatever else looked like it didn't belong there. And Devon did do the talking.

"You hear about the chicken coop?" he asked.

I shook my head.

"After Shane left here, I guess he went tearing around the streets for a while. Just laying down rubber. Then out into the country. Scary, man."

I nodded.

"So he's out west of town, past the Conoco, past the corn fields, way out by Higby's place. You know that old guy, Higby?"

I nodded. He was a kooky old chicken farmer who once brought his shotgun to a game. He got a little mixed up about where he was sometimes.

"Well, Shane gets it in his head he's going to do some damage. Wreck something, you know? So he ran off the road and across Higby's field and plowed right through one of Higby's chicken coops. Pow! Feathers everywhere. Wood and nails and eggs flying through the air. Shane tries to keep going, but he gets stuck in the mud."

"Ghaing!" I said. *Dang!*

"I know, right? Well don't worry."

I looked at him like, What?

"He called Coach Z, and Coach came to get him and talked Higby out of shooting him or calling the cops or anything. That's what I heard, anyway. From Orlando, who heard it from Shane. Sounds like it's all taken care of."

"Kaken kay augh?"

"Yeah, taken care of," Devon said. "They pulled his Chevy out of the mud and towed it home. Shane's sleeping it off now, I guess. When he wakes up, it's life as usual." Devon looked at his watch. "Assuming he makes it to practice. Lucky sucker."

Devon and I piled our garbage bags by the back door. He started squirting glass cleaner on the counters, tables, and linoleum floor. We each grabbed a wad of paper towels and started wiping.

Lucky sucker, I thought.

9/MONDAY, SEPTEMBER 23—
COACH Z'S OFFICE

On Monday, I was still wearing the bandages but I could talk. I went to Coach Z's office before practice to let him know I couldn't suit up for one more day.

"I'll be ready tomorrow," I said.

"I appreciate your dedication," Coach replied. When I didn't leave right away, he said, "Anything else, Jayo?"

"Well," I said. "There is one more thing."

He raised his eyebrows, like, Come on, let it out.

"Well, uh—is it true that Shane crashed through Higby's chicken coop? That he was driving drunk?"

"Where did you hear that?"

"I just want to know if it's true."

Coach took a few seconds before responding. "I'm guessing you know the answer to that already."

"Here's what I know," I said. And I showed him the footage of Shane getting into his car and driving away.

"Give me that," he said, reaching for the phone.

I handed it over. "I already posted it onto a private YouTube channel, if you're thinking you'll erase it. I figure I'll send the link to Principal Donahue."

Coach went over and shut his office door and sat on the desk. He lowered his voice. "Why would you want to do a thing like that, son?"

"You said everyone deserves a second chance," I said. "*One* second chance. Fine. But this is his second time drunk driving that we know of. He's been drinking at school, he's been late for practice, missing practice. He's been ignoring the rules for years. When a person messes up, there's a price to pay. At least there's supposed to be."

"You think Shane's some kind of golden boy?" he asked.

"Sure seems like it, Coach."

"You think he's had everything handed to him on a platter?" Coach asked.

"I don't know. Yeah, sort of."

"And you want to get him in trouble so you can start a football game."

"He's had his chances," I said. "Where's *my* chance?"

He handed back my phone, and I put it in my pocket. He was staring me down. Challenging me. I chose my next words carefully. "I just want to see the right thing done."

"You just want to see the right thing done."

"Yes, sir."

"Tell me something," Coach said. "When was the last time you were out to Shane's house?"

"We're not really friends anymore, Coach."

"When was the last time?"

"I don't know," I said. "Middle school?"

Shane lived out near the bus station—the roughest part of town. My family wasn't rich by any means, but I didn't find myself over in that part of Troy very often.

"Why don't you pay him a visit?"

"All due respect, sir, but I don't have anything to say to him."

"You're about to ruin a guy's career," Coach said. "You ought to go to his home and look him in the eye. Tell him what the right thing is. Don't worry about me, Jayo. Your video can't hurt me—not at this school."

He let that sink in for a minute. Then he told me to get out of his office, which I did in a hurry.

10/MONDAY, SEPTEMBER 23— GARY'S HOUSE

Mom called me that night. I was in my room doing my trig homework, only not really. Really, I was trying to decide what to do about the video. Part of me wanted to put Shane in his place. Shut him up for once. Show everyone what I could do as QB1.

But part of me didn't feel comfortable. Coach had used the words "ruin a guy's career." Would that really happen? I was leaning toward deleting the video when my phone started vibrating. Mom's name appeared on the screen.

"Hey, Mom," I said.

"Hey, honey. How are you?"

It was good to hear her voice. I missed her a lot. She'd stayed with Dad after she caught him with some other woman. And she'd stayed with him after she found out about *another* woman. She gave him second chances, even though I could see how badly it hurt her. But after the third time, she left to live with her sister.

The plan was for me to join her after classes ended last year. Then Dad got diagnosed. Mom and I got tested right away, and we were clean. And I made a tough decision: I couldn't leave him alone without any support. He was terrified and sick. He needed me more than Mom did.

Of course, Mom wanted me with her, but she said she understood. I knew she worried about me being exposed at home, even though we were very careful. Sometimes I thought she didn't want me to be exposed to *him*—not the disease.

"Guess what?" she said.

"What?"

"I'm coming to Troy for the game on Friday."

"No joke?"

"No joke, mister. Daniel is starting at linebacker for Harvest Valley, so Janet and I decided to make the trip. I'll be there for the pep rally and the game." Janet was her sister—also a recently divorced mom. Daniel was my younger cousin.

"That's great. Are you staying overnight? Can you come over for breakfast on Saturday?"

Mom sighed. "You know I can't come over, honey."

"Come on, I'll make French toast! I'll hardly get to see you Friday what with the game and everything."

"Let's go out to breakfast," she said. "You and me. OK?"

"I know Dad would like to see you, Mom."

"Honey, I'm sorry. I don't want to see him."

"OK," I said. "I love you, Mom."

11/WEDNESDAY, SEPTEMBER 25—
TROY CENTRAL HIGH

They knew about the video.

At least I thought they did. Everyone I talked to seemed to look at me weird. Some kids—Shane's friends—looked disgusted. Others gave me an extra smile of encouragement. Shane definitely had enemies at school, and I'm sure none of them would mind seeing him get taken down.

At practice, Shane still got the first-team reps, and I still got squat. If Coach Z thought there was a chance I'd be starting, he wasn't showing it. He wasn't hedging his bets at all. It was like he *knew* I didn't have the courage to turn that video over.

As for Shane, he just ignored me. If he knew that I could ruin his career, he didn't say anything about it. He didn't say anything at all.

On Wednesday after school, Orlando threw a shoulder into me as we passed in the hall. The hall was nearly empty, so there was no reason for him to pass that close. As I rolled off the hit, Joe Blatnik, middle linebacker, came up and grabbed my shirt. He and Orlando pushed me around the corner, into the darkened science hall. Joe held me against the wall.

"What do you want?" I said.

"Shut up," Orlando said.

I knocked Joe's hand away from my shirt and started to step away. He grabbed me again, harder, and slammed me into the wall.

"I would wail on you right now," Joe said.

"But for some reason, Shane don't want me to."

"He says you don't have the stones to do anything with that video," Orlando said.

"But if it somehow makes it to Donahue's office . . ." Joe said.

"Ain't nobody can protect you" Orlando said. "Got it?"

I got it all right. As they walked away, I caught my breath—I didn't realize I'd been holding it. I knew what Joe said was true: He'd love to beat the daylights out of me, and not just because of the video. He was that kind of guy. But it made me angry that he and Orlando took the time to threaten me if they weren't going to follow through.

As I thought about that, my anger started to boil over. I ran through the other things that had happened that week. Coach Z basically daring me to turn over that video. Shane ignoring me, convinced that he was safe. My dad, who wanted so badly for me to start. And finally, the fact that Mom was coming to see the game—I really wanted to play for her.

I added it all up like one big math problem, and there was only one answer: I was going to send the video into Principal Donahue. I'd show Orlando and Joe that they couldn't scare me. I'd show Coach Z he was wrong about me. I'd make my parents proud.

But first, I had to check the pulse of the locker room. I knew I had a few friends. And I knew some of the guys were tired of Shane's hotshot act. If I went to war with him, I needed to know who would be on my side.

I knew one thing: Everyone believed that winning the game against Harvest Valley was more important than any personal stuff. Winning always was. So I'd be safe until after I made the start.

After practice, while we were dressing in the locker room, I spotted Shane at the end of my row.

"Yo, Shane!" I called out. "What are those, chicken feathers in your hair?"

OK, I admit it. As a chicken coop joke, the line was pretty weak. But I knew Shane would get it right away, and so would everyone else.

Shane looked at me, but he didn't make a move. Then I heard Ernie laughing in the next row over.

"Bawk! Bawk!" he called—making a chicken noise.

A few other guys laughed.

"Don't egg him on," somebody by Ernie said.

"I'm only yolking," Ernie said.

Oh, man, these were some bad jokes. But Shane had steam coming out of his ears.

Devon shook his head. "Dude. I knew I should never have told you about that."

"Seems like you told a lot of people," I said.

Shane pulled his shirt on, slammed his locker shut, and hurried out without showering.

12/WEDNESDAY, SEPTEMBER 25—
GARY'S HOUSE

That night, I sat at my computer to work on the e-mail to Principal Donahue. I wrote it, read it over, deleted it, and wrote it again. I had trouble finding the right words. I wanted it to sound mature. Like a concerned citizen doing the responsible thing—and not like some kid tattling.

Plus, I was nervous. Once I sent this e-mail, everything was going to change. Mostly the change would be good, but it wouldn't be easy. Who knew what Shane would do? He'd definitely blow up in some unpredictable way. And he'd sure never talk to me again. Our friendship, what was left of it, would be toast.

And of course I'd be starting for the Trojans. That would mean a ton of pressure on the field and off. Coach would never forgive me. The guys on the team, some of them would never forgive me either. Orlando and Joe would come at me. I'd have to talk to the press after games, just like Shane did. He loved the attention, but I was more of a quiet type.

"Hey, Gary, what's for dinner?"

That was Dad out in the living room. Things would be different with him, too, of course. I'd have to work harder at football, leaving me less time to help him. And he'd be all over me, wanting to review plays and watch video of upcoming opponents.

I yelled down the hall: "One second, Dad!"

Finally I wrote a short and simple e-mail to the principal:

Dear Mr. Donahue. This video shows Shane Hunter driving drunk. This is a clear violation of district and team policy, which he has already previously broken before. I hope you will do the right thing and suspend him from the team.

Sincerely, Gary Jayo.

I pasted in the link to the private YouTube channel where I'd uploaded it and hit Send. Then I made dinner for my dad.

13/THURSDAY, SEPTEMBER 26—
MEDIA ROOM

After the weekly video yearbook meeting, Shane's girlfriend, Jenny, wanted to talk to me.

"I heard about this video you have," she said. We were alone in the media center—the rest of the staff had already left.

"What did you hear?" I said. The first thing I thought of was the clip of Shane with Shawna. I'd forgotten about it until now, and for a second, I felt awful. If she knew, it would hurt her badly. But then I realized she must have meant the clip of Shane getting into his truck and driving away drunk. It seemed like everyone knew about it even though nobody had seen it but Ernie and me. And probably Principal Donahue by now, too.

"I heard he was a jerk to you," Jenny said.

"Yeah, well, what else is new?"

"I heard he broke your jaw."

"Dislocated it."

"And I heard you recorded him driving away," Jenny said. "Drunk."

"So, what's up?" I asked.

"Gary, how could you do that?"

"You just said he was a jerk to me."

"So that means you'd let him risk his life?"

"His life? I thought we were talking about his career."

Jenny shook her head. I thought she was about to start crying, so I put a hand on her shoulder. "Jenny, is everything OK? Look, I don't want to hurt him. Well, maybe part of me does. Mostly I just want a level playing field."

"Wow," Jenny said. "I thought you were supposed to be smart."

And then it hit me. She wondered why I hadn't stopped him from driving drunk. That would have been the right thing to do.

"I'm sorry, Jenny, I . . ." I felt myself getting all nervous like I did with Coach Z. I hated myself all of a sudden. "I, uh—shoot, I'm sorry. That was wrong."

She was totally crying now. Something else was going on.

"Hey, what's the matter?" I asked.

She sobbed and stepped into my arms.

"Gary, was there another girl with Shane? At that party?"

"I, uh . . ."

She looked me in the eyes. She was really beautiful. "It was Shawna, wasn't it?" she said. Then she shook her head. "Never mind. Don't tell me. I'll ask him myself."

"Uh, OK," I said stupidly.

She pulled a tissue from a box on the desk and blew her nose with a cute little honk.

"He talks about you sometimes, you know," she said. "About when you guys were kids. He's never had a better friend."

"Come on," I said. "He doesn't care about me anymore. For years, all he's done is dump on me."

"I guess," she said. "He's insecure." She blew her nose again. "Anyway, I thought you'd like to know that."

That night, I drove Dad's Honda over to Shane's house. I parked along the curb, trying to decide if I'd go up and knock.

I wasn't sure why Coach Z wanted me to pay Shane a visit. I looked at the run-down house, the dangling garage door, and the weeds and garbage all over the lawn.

I thought about what Coach had said—what it meant to tell Shane what the "right thing" was. Shane didn't know where his dad was. His father had left the family years ago. His mom was an alcoholic and was into who knew what—all kind of drugs. His little sister . . . wow, she had to be in middle school these days. She looked up to him. Shane had a chance to make it big. He had a chance to get them away from all this.

The front door opened up, and Shane stepped out onto the porch to look at me.

"Gary?" he said.

I held a hand up to wave.

"What do you want?" he said.

I wasn't sure. What was I doing there? As I let my hand down, his little sister came up behind him in the doorway and looked out at me.

"That him?" I heard her say.

Something told me I'd better turn the car on, so I twisted the ignition and dropped the transmission into drive. Shane's sister was dashing across the lawn toward me. She'd picked up a rock about the size of a potato, and she was reaching back like she was going to throw it—hard.

"Hannah, don't!" Shane said.

I hit the gas and peeled out of there just as the rock slammed into the back window, spider-webbing it.

A group of guys hanging out at the Conoco station didn't even look up when they heard the crashing sound. Just another night in the neighborhood.

I drove a few blocks and then pulled over and checked YouTube on my phone. The video still only had one view, which I knew was me. Nobody else had clicked the link, which meant Principal Donahue hadn't seen the video. I logged into my account and deleted it.

14/FRIDAY, SEPTEMBER 27— GAME DAY

The halls were crazy with banners and posters that blared *Go Trojans!* and *Destroy Harvest Valley!* and stuff like that. From first period on, the students were pumped up and rowdy, and most of the teachers kind of gave up even trying to get anything done.

We had a big pep rally during fourth period, with the band playing and teachers performing a funny sketch about life at Troy High. Principal Donahue played Shane in the sketch, and he was pretty funny. He walked around with his chin in the air singing Eminem lyrics, which got a good laugh out of everyone, even Shane. I felt a little relieved—after that display, I was sure Donahue hadn't seen the video.

There were some alumni in the gym, too, including my mom and Aunt Janet. When the football team came out on the floor, everyone cheered like crazy, especially the alumni. Mom put her fingers in her mouth and let out a long whistle. My heart sank a little, since I wouldn't be able to play for her. But oh well. She knew I wasn't a starter. She hadn't come down here to see me start. She had come to see *me*.

After school, I ran home and took a shower. When I came out, Dad was sitting on the couch.

"Taking a shower *before* your game?" he said. It was kind of weird, I admit. But Dad knew why I was doing it—he just wanted me to say it.

"I'm getting a quick dinner with Mom before I have to head back to school. She's in town, you know."

"I heard that," he said, staring at the TV. He had another nature show on, something with a guy trying to survive alone in the wild. He wouldn't look at me.

"Dad, I—"

"Have fun," he said.

"Do you . . . do you want to come?"

"Ha. You know your mom wouldn't appreciate that."

"Well."

"It's OK," Dad said. "Go on. I mean it."

"All right. I'll see you after the game?"

He sat there watching TV for a minute, and I stood by the door, waiting. The guy on TV was talking to the camera, which must have been attached to his backpack or something: "You can get water condensation out of leaves if you know how to extract it."

"Dad?"

He looked at me. "I guess I'm going to miss the game, son. I'm really not feeling very well. The meds are acting up tonight."

Dad had only ever gotten sick from his meds in the morning, so I was a little surprised. But all I said was, "OK."

"Not like I'll be missing anything anyway," he said. Because I wasn't starting, he meant. All I would be doing is holding on extra points and field goals. Not too much fun for a dad who'd spent his life in Troy, worshipping Trojan football.

"OK," I said again. "Get some rest, Dad."

Mom texted me to let me know she was on her way, so I picked up my football gear and waited for her at the end of the driveway.

15/FRIDAY, SEPTEMBER 27—
GAME DAY

"Your Troy Central High School Trojans!" the announcer called over the loudspeaker. We ran out of the stadium tunnel, new this season, and burst through a banner.

A few players held their helmets above their heads like weapons. The crowd screamed, the band played, and the lights blazed. Pretty much the whole town was in attendance, and half of Harvest Valley too.

The Harvest Valley Millers had a good, stout defense, but that wouldn't be too much of a problem for us. Shane and the guys could play their game against anybody. The bigger weapon they had was a dangerous power running game. Their fullback, Anton LaBelle, was built like a truck. He cleared out holes for their running back, Lance "Lightning" Shroder, who was as strong as a Clydesdale and as fast as one too. And they had an offensive line that could move a house if it was in the way. You could expect a steady dose of Lightning all night long.

When the Trojans lined up for the kickoff, the crowd got amped up again. You could feel electricity in the air as the ball tumbled end over end toward the Harvest Valley return man. When the Trojan defense laid him out at the twelve-yard line, everyone exploded.

But then Harvest Valley began to hammer its way up the field. LaBelle and Lightning, right up the middle, time after time. And it was working. Hand off to Lightning. Hand off to Lightning again. Why mess with a good thing?

The quarterback hardly had to do anything, just hand off. And I started to daydream a little bit. Man, if Harvest Valley had a quarterback with more talent—somebody like me—they'd be unstoppable.

We would be unstoppable.

I don't know why I was torturing myself like that. I'd made up my mind to stay in Troy with my dad. I had friends in town. I'd put in a lot of work on the video yearbook. I was happy, mostly. I'd had my chance to go to Harvest Valley last summer and declined.

It didn't look like they needed my help, anyway. Their drive chewed more than seven minutes off the clock and resulted in a touchdown. Just like that, the crackle of energy in the stadium became a soft buzz.

As special teams lined up to take the kickoff, Shane walked over to me. He didn't usually talk to people during games. And he hadn't talked to me at all for a week.

"You bring your A game tonight?" he said, looking out at the field.

"Don't worry," I said. "I'll be an all-pro holder."

"I know about the video you took of me. Coach Z said you wanted to show it to Donahue."

"Well, I didn't do it," I said.

"I know. If you did, I wouldn't be standing here."

"I guess."

We were still both only looking at the field. It's hard for guys like us to look at each other when saying something nice. Terry caught the kickoff and dodged a tackler. He was crossing the thirty with momentum.

"I bet it was a hard decision," Shane said. "The way I've been acting, I bet you were dying to cut me down."

After Terry got tackled at the thirty-six, Shane finally looked at me. "I hope you brought *all* your skills tonight, brother."

He hit me on the back and ran out onto the

field with the rest of the offense.

Troy's first offensive play was a pitch to Devon, who galloped around the right side. Ernie sealed off the end, and Devon burst upfield for eight yards.

Coach loves to call a post or deep slant on second and short, and that's what he did. Shane lined up behind center and shouted out the count. He took the snap, stepped back, and faked a handoff to Devon. Devon quickly picked up a block on my cousin, Daniel, who had gotten behind the line.

Shane looked downfield. He had Orlando open, but instead of hitting him for an easy big gain, he tucked the ball and ran around the end—on Ernie's side again. Ernie did his job and blocked the cornerback who was on the spot. Shane flew past them. The strong safety was closing in fast.

Normally, Shane would juke that guy out of his shoes and leave him diving toward the ground, reaching at Shane's vapor trail. Instead, he let up a bit, opened his chest, and took the hit.

Oof.

He went down, and hard. The Troy cheering section groaned in unison. The Harvest Valley fans let out their inner hater and cheered. An injured Trojan—hurray! Not only that, it was Shane Hunter, legendary quarterback.

The key to the Troy offense.

Coach and Gus, the trainer, ran onto the field fast. Shane moved his legs around, but he wasn't getting up.

Coach Z and Gus hovered around Shane for a few minutes, until he began to rise. The crowd cheered, the way you do when you want to let a hurt player know you're glad he's OK. Shane wobbled dramatically as he came off the field.

I watched him closely. As he reached the sideline, helmet off, he looked dazed. I heard one of the coaches say "concussion symptoms." But when Shane caught my eye, I swear to God he winked.

There was no time to figure out what had just happened, because I was in the game. I grabbed a ball and started throwing with one of our cornerbacks. Then everyone gathered around Coach.

"No change to the game plan!" he was yelling. "Jayo can do everything on this play sheet. Let's go out there, now, and show them whose house they're in!"

Orlando grabbed the collar of my jersey and got in close to my face.

"Don't screw this up, backup," he whispered.

"Let's go!" Coach yelled.

We ran out onto the field. The whole stadium was swimming around me. I had to get a hold of my thoughts.

I tried to remember the game plan, but everything was blank. I stood in the huddle, and the guys looked at me.

"What's the play, Gary?" It was Ernie.

What was the play? Coach Z had just told me, and I'd forgotten. I looked out at the sideline, and he was standing there watching us. Shane, sitting on the bench, nodded. Across the field, the Harvest Valley defense stood waiting.

It was third and two. First things first. We needed to get a first down.

I called a quick slant to Orlando.

We lined up, and I took the snap. Three-step drop, fire.

The cornerback had Orlando covered pretty tight, but I thought I could wedge the football in there. I was wrong. My cousin knocked the ball to the ground.

"What was that?" Coach yelled at me when we came off. The punting unit took the field, getting ready to do its thing.

"Sorry, Coach. I blanked on the play. I thought they'd expect a cold QB to come in and hand it off, so I tried something different."

"Don't try something different," Coach said.

"Yes, Coach. I got this. Don't worry."

"A little late for don't worry, Jayo."

Harvest Valley put together another nice long drive, but they stalled on the nine and settled for a field goal. It was ten–zero, and the first quarter was about over.

After the kickoff, we started out across the

thirty again. Devon gained us nine yards during a couple of run plays. On third-and-one, I fired a quick out to Ernie for a first down.

All right. I was settling in.

Next play was another hand off to Devon, but this time, he was stuffed at the line—by Daniel. My cousin was having a heck of a game already. On second-and-ten, we ran the same play, and the Millers stuffed Devon again for a loss of two.

I threw to Terry on third-and-twelve, but a defender tipped my pass. The ball wobbled out into the flat and the Harvest Valley CB intercepted it. Terry wrapped him up right away, but our defense did not look happy to be coming out on the field again.

"Gary!" Shane called me over. "The LBs and safeties are cheating in, man." The Millers' defense was selling out to defend the run because they didn't expect me to do anything through the air. "You gotta make them pay for that," he said.

"I know," I said. "But Coach is calling

runs. He doesn't trust me."

"So change the plays. You're the QB. Do what you and I both know you can do."

"You seem OK to me," I said. "Maybe you should come back in."

Shane smiled. "Can't. I told Coach I'm groggy. He's not letting me back in."

During the next set of downs, our defense shut down the Millers' running attack, a three-and-out. After the punt, we had the ball on our own thirty-four. Coach called all running plays again. We got one first down, but then we had to kick it.

When Harvest Valley got the ball back, LaBelle and Lightning started gashing holes through the line. Our D was getting tired—they'd been on the field for most of the first half. The Millers moved easily down the field and scored another touchdown. We were down by seventeen in a home game we should have been in control of.

Not good.

The Trojan offense was stunned. The

Trojan defense was gasping for air. The crowd was nervous.

We got the ball back with less than two minutes in the half. Coach wanted another run up the middle on first-and-ten.

I looked up and saw my mom in the stands cheering. I thought of my dad at home listening on the radio.

Why not, I thought. I called play-action instead.

I took the snap. Devon came running toward me, and I faked the handoff. Shane was right— the entire Harvest Valley defense was crowding the line. I looked over their helmets and saw Orlando crossing on that slant. This time, I hit him in stride, and he caught it. Twenty-two yard gain.

Next I called play-action again and hit Ernie on a curl. Gain of nine. I could almost see the Harvest Valley defense softening up. They had to respect the pass all of the sudden, so we ran a trap, and Devon ripped off a huge gain.

The Troy crowd was starting to get back

into the game. The guys on offense were already looking at me differently in the huddle, like they believed in me.

A couple plays later, we scored a touchdown on a hitch to Terry. We went into halftime down seventeen–seven, which felt a lot better than seventeen–zero.

Shouts filled the locker room as Coach tried to get everyone settled down and focused. Guys on defense were yelling that they needed some help—longer offensive drives so they could get a breather between possessions. All the while, Shane was talking in my ear, giving me advice. And suddenly, I realized we were going to win.

I don't just mean I had a good feeling. I don't just mean I felt confident in my abilities. I mean, I *knew* it.

We were going to win.

I'd never really been sure of anything in my life. I'd had second thoughts about staying in Troy. I'd had second thoughts about sticking at QB when I could have gotten snaps at wide receiver, at least a few as the number-three guy. I had all kinds of questions about Dad: How could he cheat on Mom like that? And why did he keep pressuring me to fight for QB1? Why couldn't he lay off?

It felt good to be sure of this one thing. We were going to win. I was going to make it happen.

We got first possession of the second half and ran a nice, balanced drive. I was four out of four passing, and Devon gained yards on the ground like he was angry. Seven minutes later, we had a touchdown, cutting the Millers' lead to three. Our defense held on the Millers' next possession, and when we got the ball back, we scored a field goal to tie it up.

It wasn't all pretty, though. I threw another interception, and the Millers took back the lead twice more. For a while, it looked like Lighting would have his way with our tired defense. But my feeling had been right.

I made enough plays to keep it close. Devon

ran like an MVP. And our defense rose to the moment. Late in the fourth quarter, our guys on D forced Lighting to cough up a fumble that gave us our chance. We moved quickly, needing a touchdown to win—a field goal would not be enough.

Finally, with time running out, I threw the winning TD.

16/FRIDAY, SEPTEMBER 27—
AFTER THE GAME

Joe Blatnik threw the big party at his house that night—his parents were out of town. Shane said I should come, but I had a date with my mom.

"Say hi to her for me," he said. He used to hang out at our house all the time when we were younger.

"I will," I said. "Actually, do you want to come?"

"No, thanks," he said. "I can't let everyone down. The boys can't have fun without me, you know."

Part of me felt like I should say thanks for taking a dive—for letting me play—but it seemed too weird. Instead, we shook hands and went our separate ways.

Mom and I went bowling, and she talked about her house and friends up in Harvest Valley. She told me about her job at the women's clinic and how much fun it was hanging out with Janet and Daniel. She told me how she wished I were there too. When she dropped me at home, she gave me a long hug.

"I'm proud of you," she said.

I went inside and got right in bed. I was drained. It had been a long, crazy, emotional day. But as soon as I turned the light off, Dad stepped in and turned it on again.

"Good game tonight," he said.

"You listened on the radio?"

"I did. What happened on that second pick? Sounded like you didn't look off the safety."

"Yeah," I said. "I guess. I'm pretty tired, Dad."

"I understand. Better get some rest. It's going to be an interesting week at practice. Coach Z is going to have a tough decision to make."

"No, he isn't."

"Sure he is, son. You played a heck of a game."

"I know. But Shane is better. He just is."

Dad sat on the edge of the bed.

"Don't sell yourself short," he said.

"I'm not. I'm selling myself exactly right. And it's OK. I'm happy the way things are."

"You had a taste of the glory," he said. "Didn't you like it?"

"I did. I liked it a lot. But a taste is all I need."

He looked down at his hands. Thinking again. "We'll talk about it tomorrow," he said.

"There's nothing else to talk about," I said. I mustered up my courage. "You need to let it go, Dad."

He looked like I'd slapped him. "What do you mean let it go?"

"Let me be my own person."

He sat still for a minute. Finally, he said, "Well, good night, then."

"I love you, Dad."

He nodded as he walked out of the room.

Even though I was exhausted, I had trouble sleeping. I lay awake thinking half the night. I wanted to change a few things about myself. I wanted to pick up extra shifts at the café and make more money so I could get Dad's back window fixed. And I wanted to buy my own car so I could visit Mom at least a couple times a month. I decided I'd commit to a university out of state that had strong academics and an unimportant division-two football team. Those were all things I could control—ways to make my life better.

But the main thing I kept thinking about was the end of that night's football game. I liked that part a lot.

We'd been down thirty-one–twenty-seven, with half a minute left on the clock. We had the ball at the Harvest Valley thirty-eight.

Coach called for Orlando to run a fly pattern—he was the primary target on this play. If he was open, I had to hit him. I took a seven-step drop and scanned the field. Orlando had beaten his guy and had separation heading to the end zone. But I didn't throw it to him. I pump-faked his way, and the Harvest Valley safety bit, stepping toward him. That left Ernie open on the other side, and I threw it his way. It was a beautiful pass, a tight spiral that shined under the stadium lights. The whole stadium watched along with me as Ernie reached out his big arms, caught it, and ran it in for the win.

ABOUT THE AUTHOR

Herman Brown is a writer from Minneapolis.

THE RED ZONE

WINNING IS *NOT OPTIONAL.*

OUT OF THE TUNNEL

BREAKTHROUGH

THE OPTION

AT ALL COSTS

TAKE AWAY

RISE ABOVE

THE **CATCH**

FORCED **OUT**

HIGH **HEAT**

OUT OF **CONTROL**

POWER **HITTER**

THE **PROSPECT**

LOOK FOR THESE
TITLES FROM THE

TRAVEL TEAM

COLLECTION.

WELCOME TO

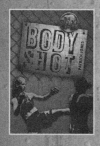

LEARN TO FIGHT,
LEARN TO LIVE,
AND LEARN
TO FIGHT
FOR YOUR
LIFE.

archenemy

As a defender for Fraser High, Addie used to be ready for anything. But now the biggest threat on the field is her former best friend.

the beast

When a concussion takes Alyssa out of the lineup, her rising-star teammate Becca takes over in goal. Will Alyssa heal in time for playoffs? And how far will she go to reclaim the goalie jersey?

blow out

Lacy spent the winter recovering from a knee injury that still gives her nightmares. Now Raven is going after her starting spot. Can Lacy get past her fears and play the way she used to?

offside

It might be crazy, but Faith has a crush on her coach. Can she keep her head in the game? And when Faith's frenemy Caitlyn decides that Faith's getting special treatment, will Faith become an outcast?

out of sync

Since childhood, Madison and Dayton have had soccer sync. But lately, Dayton is more interested in partying than playing soccer. Can Maddie get through to her best friend?

under pressure

Taking "performance supplements" makes Elise feel great, and lately she's been playing like a powerhouse. But will it last? How long can she keep the pills a secret?